With love and thanks to Richard and Roger.

Here's Pip. He's wearing his hat backwards.
Can you spot him on every page?

First published in Great Britain in 2005 by Chrysalis Children's Books,
an imprint of Chrysalis Books Group Plc
The Chrysalis Building, Bramley Road, London W10 6SP
www.chrysalisbooks.co.uk

This edition produced by Inky Press Ltd, UK, BN7 2NZ
Text copyright © Jill Lewis 2005
Illustrations, design and layout copyright © Inky Press 2005

The moral right of the author has been asserted.

A CIP catalogue record for this book is available from the British Library.

ISBN 1 84458 376 7

Printed in China

2 4 6 8 10 9 7 5 3 1

This book can be ordered direct from the publisher. Please contact
the Marketing Department. But try your bookshop first.

# A Mum in a Million

written by
Jill Lewis

illustrated by
Stephen Gulbis

Chrysalis Children's Books

It was Pip's first day at school. But he didn't want to go.
So after breakfast, he hid.

"Come out, Pip!" said Mrs Penguin. "All little penguins go to school.
You'll learn how to make water holes in the ice and catch fish."

Mrs Penguin found Pip and gave him his school bag.

"At school, all little penguins learn to slide
and make ice carvings," she said.

But Pip still didn't want to go to school.

"What IS the matter, Pip?" said Mrs Penguin.

"All penguins look the same!" cried Pip. "When school's over, how will I find you?"

Mrs Penguin wiped away Pip's tears. She smiled.

"Don't worry, chick," she said. "Miss Peck wrote to all the penguin parents. You'll be able to find me as soon as school finishes, I promise."

Dear Mums & Dads,
Please make sure your chick can find you after school. There is a medal for the parent who stands out best from the crowd!
Primrose Peck (Miss)

As soon as she got home, Mrs Penguin set to work. She hammered and snipped and painted. By the afternoon, she had finished.

Pip loved his first day at school. All the little penguins learned how to make water holes in the ice. Then they learned how to catch fish.

At home time, Pip looked eagerly for his mum. But every single penguin parent had had the same idea. They were ALL holding big signs with messages for their chicks.

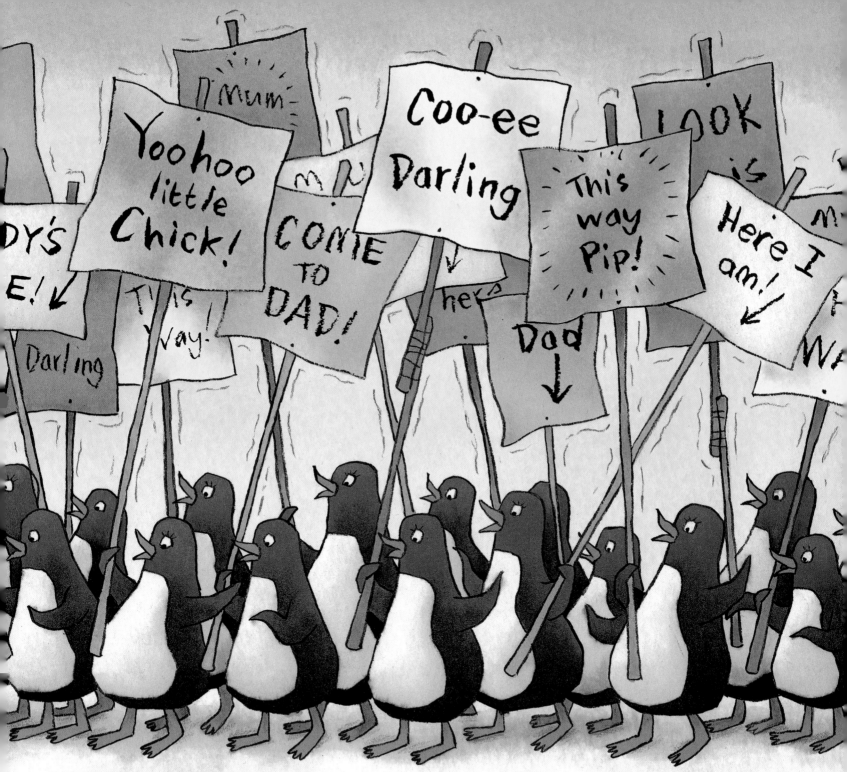

Pip found his mum at last.

"Don't worry, chick," said Mrs Penguin.
"I have a better idea. You'll be able to find me tomorrow, I promise."

That night, Mrs Penguin waited until Pip was tucked up in bed.
Then she set to work again. She knitted and stitched and snipped.
By ten o'clock, she had finished.

At school the next day, Pip learned how to slide on the ice.

At home time, Pip looked anxiously for his mum. Oh, no! This time, ALL the penguin parents were wearing brightly coloured knitted hats!

Pip found his mum at last.

"Don't worry, chick," said Mrs Penguin.
"I have a much better idea. You'll be able to find me tomorrow, I promise."

That night, Mrs Penguin waited until Pip was fast asleep.
Then she set to work again. She sawed and sanded and hammered.
By midnight, she had finished.

At school the next day, Pip learned how to make ice carvings.
He carved an icy Miss Peck.

At home time, Pip just stared and stared. ALL the penguin parents were towering high above him on stilts. But which one was his mum?

Pip found Mrs Penguin at last.

"Don't worry, chick," she said. "Tomorrow, I'll make sure
I stand out from the crowd, I promise."

That night, Mrs Penguin had the best idea ever.

"Why didn't I think of this before?" she chuckled.

She didn't hammer, snip, paint, knit, stitch, saw or sand.
Instead, she went straight to bed.

At school the next day, Pip learned how to slide
and swirl and twirl on the ice.

At home time, all the little penguins rushed out. The crowd of penguin parents was there to meet them. They were all in fancy dress – except for Mrs Penguin, who was dressed as...

...A PENGUIN!

"You win the medal, Mrs Penguin!" said Miss Peck.

"For being a mum in a million," said Pip.